POSEY ON PARADE!

"Why can't everyone wear whatever they want to school?" Posey said bravely.

Miss Lee stood up. She squeezed her lips together and thought.

"Well, I guess because then we'd have pirates and clowns and super-heroes and ballet dancers in our class," she said at last.

"What's wrong with that?" said Posey.

"That doesn't sound very much like a first-grade class, does it?" said Miss Lee.

"No," said Posey. "It sounds like a parade."

Enjoy all the books starring
PRINCESS P✿SEY, FIRST GRADER

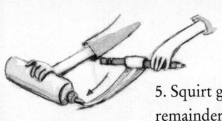

5. Squirt glue onto the remainder of the triangle.

6. Carefully roll the pencil right up to the tip.

7. Slip the bead off and stand it upright to dry.

8. Paint your beads with clear nail polish to make them shiny! Or use sparkly nail polish to make them fancy!

9. String your beads onto your necklace.

That's all you have to do! I'm going to ask Miss Lee if I can show the whole class.

Love, Posey

P. S. I painted my beads with sparkly purple nail polish. They're beautiful!!!

PRINCESS POSEY

Now that you've read the first three, be sure to make reading sparkle with these other great books!

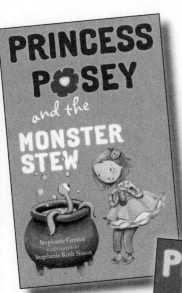

PRINCESS
POSEY
and the
MONSTER
STEW

Stephanie Greene
ILLUSTRATED BY
Stephanie Roth Sisson

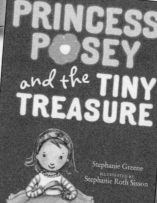

PRINCESS
POSEY
and the TINY
TREASURE

Stephanie Greene
ILLUSTRATED BY
Stephanie Roth Sisson

A Pocketful of
PRINCESS POSEY

Princess Posey Books 1–3

PRINCESS POSEY
and the
FIRST GRADE PARADE

PRINCESS POSEY
and the
PERFECT PRESENT

PRINCESS POSEY
and the
NEXT–DOOR DOG

PUFFIN BOOKS
An Imprint of Penguin Group (USA)

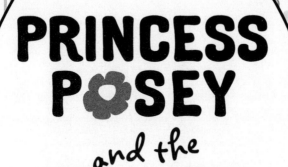

PRINCESS
P✿SEY

and the

FIRST GRADE
PARADE

Stephanie Greene

ILLUSTRATED BY
Stephanie Roth Sisson

PUFFIN BOOKS
Published by the Penguin Group
Penguin Group (USA) LLC
375 Hudson Street
New York, New York 10014

USA * Canada * UK * Ireland * Australia
New Zealand * India * South Africa * China

penguin.com
A Penguin Random House Company

First published in the United States of America by G. P. Putnam's Sons,
a division of Penguin Young Readers Group, 2010
Published by Puffin Books, a division of Penguin Young Readers Group, 2011
This omnibus edition published by Puffin Books,
an imprint of Penguin Young Readers Group, 2014

Text copyright © 2010 by Stephanie Greene
Illustrations copyright © 2010 by Stephanie Roth Sisson

THE LIBRARY OF CONGRESS HAS CATALOGED THE G. P. PUTNAM'S SONS EDITION AS FOLLOWS:
Greene, Stephanie.
Princess Posey and the first grade parade / by Stephanie Greene ;
illustrated by Stephanie Roth Sisson.
p. cm.
Summary: Posey's fear of starting first grade is alleviated when her teacher invites the
students to wear their most comfortable clothes to school on the first day.
ISBN: 978-0-339-25167-2 (hardcover)
[1. Fear—Fiction. 2. First day of school—Fiction. 3. Schools—Fiction.]
I. Sisson, Stephanie Roth, ill. II. Title
PZ7.G8434Pk 2010
[Fic]—dc22 2009012471

Puffin Books ISBN 978-0-14-241827-7

This omnibus edition ISBN 978-0-14-751472-1

Printed in the United States of America

1 3 5 7 9 10 8 6 4 2

For Ellie and Natalie —S.G.

For Trammell and Olivia —S.R.S.

CONTENTS

KISS AND GO LANE

"You're leaving me," said Posey.

"I am not leaving you," said her mom. "I am going to drop you off at the front of the school. Miss Lee will be there to meet you at your classroom door."

"It feels like you're leaving me," said Posey.

"All the first-graders walk to their rooms," her mom said. She slipped a spoonful of green peas into Danny's mouth. "You'll be fine. Eat your lunch now."

Posey didn't feel like eating. She was worried about the first day of school. It was only five days away.

Posey was going to be in first grade.

All summer long, her mom had talked about the fun things Posey was going to do. Like draw. And learn to read. And play games.

But all Posey could
think about was the sign in
front of her school.

It said, Kiss and Go Lane.

It was where Posey had to kiss
her mom good-bye.

And open the car door.

And walk into the school.

All by herself.

"Last year you didn't drop me off," Posey said. "You walked me to my class."

"Last year you were no bigger than a minute." Her mom smiled. "You're a big girl now."

"I don't want to be a big girl."

Posey got off her chair and squatted down. She wrapped her arms around her knees. "See? I'm as small as I was last year."

Danny peered at her over the edge of his high chair and laughed.

CHAPTER TWO

THE
PINK
PRINCESS

"**S**it up and finish your lunch," her mom said patiently.

Posey got back on her chair.

"Why aren't you leaving Danny?" she asked.

"I told you," her mom said. "My new job has day care."

"You *should* leave him." Posey wrinkled her nose. "He smells."

"I think he smells sweet." Her mom buried her nose in Danny's neck. He grabbed her hair.

Posey felt the ends of her mouth turn down. "You love Danny more than me," she said.

"Oh, Posey."

Her mom came around the table. She put her arm around Posey's stiff shoulders. "It's going to be fine, sweetie. You'll see. We'll buy you something new to wear."

"Why can't I wear this?"

Posey pointed to her pink tutu. It had a hole above her belly button. The skirt had a tear on one side.

Posey loved to wear it more than anything. She wore it every day, all summer long.

It made her feel special.

Posey never told anyone, but when she wore her pink tutu, she was Princess Posey, the Pink Princess.

Princess Posey could go anywhere. Do anything.

Even walk into first grade by herself.

"You can wear it when you get home from school," said her mom.

Posey didn't want to wear it *after* school. She wanted to wear it *to* school.

Her mom untied Danny's bib.

"You wait with Danny while I get some towels," she said. "We'll go for a swim."

"It's all your fault," Posey said to Danny with a big frown. "I was the baby till you got here."

Danny smiled and grabbed his toes.

"Mom thinks you're great because you're a baby," Posey said. "But you wait."

She leaned forward until their noses were almost touching. "One day she will leave you the way she's leaving me."

Danny blew a bubble and laughed.

MONSTER
OF THE
BLUE HALL .

After Posey went swimming, she ran to the playground. Tyler and Nick were on the slide.

They lived next door to Posey. They were brothers.

"Hey, Posey!" they called.

Posey went over to them.

"Tyler and me want to make sure you're ready for first grade," Nick said.

"I'm getting new shoes," said Posey.

"You know you have to walk into the school by yourself, right?" said Tyler.

"I can do that," Posey said bravely.

"What about the hall?" asked Nick.

"What hall?" said Posey.

"The hall is long and dark," Tyler said in a spooky voice. He banged his foot on the slide.

Boom.

"You're all
by yourself."
Another
boom.

Posey looked up at him from the
bottom of the slide and shivered.

"If the monster grabs you, there's
no one around to help," said Nick.

"Monster?" said Posey. She looked from one boy to the other. "There's no monster at Middle Pond School."

"Oh, yes, there is," said Tyler. "Isn't there, Nick?"

He jabbed his younger brother in the side.

Nick nodded. "The Monster of the Blue Hall," he said.

The blue hall was for the first grade. Tyler was in the fourth grade. He was on the green hall.

Nick was on the red hall with the other second-graders.

"Most first-graders don't make it to their classrooms," Tyler said.

"The monster gets them first," said Nick. "It sucks out their blood. The rest get eaten by snakes."

"Snakes?" said Posey.

Nick and Tyler loved to tease her. They teased her all the time.

Posey knew they were teasing her now.

Still, she tightened her grip on her stuffed giraffe.

CHAPTER
FOUR

ONE WAY
TO
FIND OUT

"I never saw any snakes," said Posey.

"They don't come out for kinder-garteners," said Nick. "They only come out for first-graders."

"First-graders without their mothers," added Tyler.

Posey let out a little squeak. The boys fell against each other and laughed. They thought they were the smartest boys in the whole world.

It made Posey mad.

"How come the monster didn't get you?" she asked.

"It did," said Nick. "Didn't it, Tyler?"

Tyler nodded. "We don't have blood inside," he said.

"Everyone has blood," said Posey.

"Not Tyler and me," said Nick. "We have ink. Look."

The boys held out their wrists. Posey stared at their blue veins.

"Blood is red," Nick said in a spooky voice. "Ink is blue."

Posey knew Nick was trying to scare her. But what if what he said was true?

There was only one way to find out.

Posey picked up a stick and jabbed him.

NO SNAKES,
NO MONSTERS

Gramps came over to take Posey for a ride after dinner.

She was quiet when he pulled out of the driveway.

She was quiet when he tooted his horn two times to say good-bye to Danny.

"Cat got your tongue?" Gramps said. "You're mighty quiet tonight."

Posey shook her head. She didn't say a word.

"Your mom told me about Nick," Gramps said. "I guess you got him pretty good."

Posey stared out the window.

"Want to tell me about it?" Gramps asked.

Posey told him all about the Monster of the Blue Hall.

And the snakes.

And the first-graders
without their mothers.

The tight feeling in her chest
got looser as she talked. Gramps
reached over and patted her knee
when she was finished.

"They were pulling your leg, Posey," he said. "Blood looks blue until it hits the air. Then it's red. They were trying to scare you, that's all."

Posey looked at her arm. Her veins were blue, too. "There's no monster, is there, Gramps?" she said.

"Nope. No snakes, either. That school has been around since your mom was a little girl. No one has seen a monster yet."

It made Posey feel better to hear Gramps say it. But thinking about school still gave her a funny feeling in her stomach.

"What do you say we stop at Hank's and get an ice cream?" said Gramps.

He swung his truck into the dusty parking lot in front of a small store. He and Posey went inside.

"You go pick your flavor," said Gramps. "I want to pick up some milk."

Posey ran to the back of the store. She slid open the lid of the ice cream freezer. When she was too small to reach it, Gramps had to pull a wooden box over for her to stand on.

Now she stood on tiptoe and looked in. There were cherry, orange, and grape Popsicles. Posey picked cherry and slid the lid closed.

She started back to find Gramps.

Halfway down the aisle, Posey froze.

Miss Lee, her very own first-grade teacher, was standing at the front of the store. Posey saw her when she visited Miss Lee's class last year.

Seeing her in Hank's made Posey feel shy.

CHAPTER SIX

A MOUSE
COULD HIDE

Posey wished she was a mouse so she could hide.

What if Miss Lee saw her? What if she talked to Posey and asked her questions?

"Posey," called a loud voice. "Over here!"

It was Gramps. He was in the line next to Miss Lee.

Posey ran and hid her face against his shirt. She felt his strong arm wrap around her.

"What's all this about?" said Gramps.

Before Posey could answer, she heard another voice.

"Hello, Posey."

Posey looked up.

Miss Lee was smiling at her.

"I'm Linda Lee," she told Gramps.

"Posey's first-grade teacher."

"What do you know about that, Posey?" said Gramps. "Your teacher shops at Hank's, too."

All Posey could do was nod.

CHAPTER SEVEN

POSEY'S
IDEA

"You'll like having Posey in your class," Gramps said. "She's a good girl and a hard worker."

"I'm sure she is," said Miss Lee. "I love your tutu, Posey. I love pink, too."

Miss Lee held out her foot. She was wearing pink sneakers. They looked like they had been washed a million times.

Her pinkie toe poked out through a hole in the end.

"These old things are ready for the trash," said Miss Lee. "But I can't bear to part with them."

"Posey is the same way," said Gramps. "She would wear her ballet outfit to school every day of the year, if she could."

"I know exactly how she feels."

Miss Lee squatted down so she could look into Posey's eyes. "I bet your tutu is comfortable, isn't it?" she said.

Posey nodded.

"My shoes are, too," said Miss Lee. "It's too bad we can't wear

our favorite old clothes to school,
isn't it?"

Posey stared back at her, round-
eyed. "Why can't we?" she asked.

"Why can't we?" Miss Lee
sounded surprised.

"Why can't everyone wear what
they want to school?" Posey said
bravely.

Miss Lee stood up. She squeezed her lips together and thought.

"Well, I guess because then we'd have pirates and clowns and super-heroes and ballet dancers in our class," she said at last.

"What's wrong with that?" said Posey.

"Now, Posey . . ." said Gramps.

"It's all right," Miss Lee told him. She smiled at Posey again.

Posey thought Miss Lee was pretty.

"That doesn't sound very much

like a first-grade class, does it?" said
Miss Lee.

"No," said Posey. "It sounds like
a parade."

CHAPTER
EIGHT

THE
MAGIC VEIL

Posey couldn't sit still. The invitation had come in the morning mail.

It was for Miss Lee's "First Day of First Grade Parade."

Dear First-Graders,

My friend Posey gave me a great idea yesterday. Because you are all so different and creative, you are invited to come to school dressed in your favorite clothes. We will have a parade to start off the new school year.

WHEN: The first day of school
WHERE: Middle Pond School, front steps
TIME: 8:00 a.m.

I will be outside to greet you. We will parade down the blue hall to our class.

Sincerely,
Miss Lee

Posey's tutu was clean and almost like new. Her mom had mended the hole and the tear.

Now Gramps was coming over to give Posey a present. She bounced up and down on the couch. She ran to the window to look out.

"He's here!" she shouted when Gramps's truck pulled into the driveway. She ran outside and hugged Gramps as hard as she could.

"Hang on now." Gramps laughed. "What's all the excitement?"

Posey's mom came out onto the front porch holding Danny. "Let

Gramps get inside," she called.

In the living room, Gramps handed Posey a shiny box with a silver bow.

"Go on, open it," he said.

Inside was a beautiful pink veil covered with stars. Posey held it up.

The stars sparkled like magic. They were blue and green and red.

"Put it on," said Gramps. "Let's see how it looks."

The veil fell around Posey's shoulders like a cloud.

A sparkly pink cloud.

Posey started to
twirl. She twirled
and twirled as if
she would never
stop.

"Posey, slow
down," said her mom.

But Posey couldn't slow down.

She was Princess Posey,

the Pink Princess.

Princess Posey

was

floating.

Around and
around and around
like a dream.

When Posey bumped into the couch, Gramps put his arms around her.

"You know what makes that veil so magic?" he said.

"What?"

"You and that brave heart of yours. It's all you will ever need."

Posey knew Gramps was right.

CHAPTER NINE

POOR DANNY

"Poor Danny," Posey said as she got into bed. "He can't go to first grade tomorrow."

She curled up on her side so she could look at her veil. It was hanging on the back of her chair.

"How about a book?" said her mom.

"Not tonight," said Posey. "I want to fall asleep fast so it's tomorrow."

Her mom sat on the edge of Posey's bed.

"Now, remember," she said. "Tomorrow I'm going to stop the car at the Kiss and Go sign."

Posey nodded.

"You'll give me a kiss and walk up to the school, okay?"

"Miss Lee will be waiting," said Posey.

"Right."

"Miss Lee smiles a lot," Posey said sleepily.

"I'm glad," said her mom.

Her mom kissed her good night and turned off the light. But Posey didn't close her eyes.

She wanted to see if her veil sparkled in the dark.

It did.

With every new breeze that came through

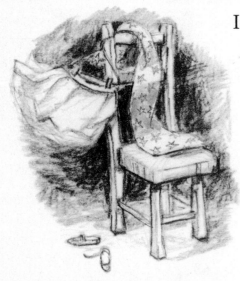

the window, the stars twinkled in the light of the moon.

Right up to the minute Posey fell asleep.

Right on through the night.

They were twinkling in the sun the next morning when she opened her eyes.

It was the first day of first grade.

CHAPTER TEN

TICKLED PINK

The line of cars inched forward.

"Hurry, Mom, hurry!" Posey begged. She could hardly wait to reach the Kiss and Go Lane sign.

The minute they did, she opened her door.

"How about a kiss?" said her mom.

Posey gave her a kiss and got out of the car. There were children everywhere. Posey saw a cowboy. Then Miss Lee's smiling face.

"How about Danny?" her mom called.

"Bye-bye, Danny!" Posey cried. She blew him a kiss and ran toward Miss Lee.

Miss Lee was surrounded by children. They didn't look like

they were dressed for school at all!
Posey saw a girl in her pajamas and
a boy in a soccer uniform. Another
boy wore huge dinosaur slippers.

There was even a girl wearing a
tutu.

Her tutu was blue.

"I wish I had a veil with sparkles,"
she said.

Miss Lee put her hands on Posey's shoulders.

"All right, everyone," she called. "I want you all to line up behind Posey."

Everyone rushed to get in line.
The cowboy was first behind Posey.
Then the girl in the blue tutu. She
had curly blond hair.

She smiled at Posey.

Posey smiled back.

The line was wiggling and
squirming like a worm. Miss Lee
held up her hand.

"Listen carefully," she said. "We
are going to march into the school
and down the blue hall to our room.
Is everybody ready?"

"READY!" shouted the worm.

"Follow Posey," said Miss Lee. "She's the leader today."

So Miss Lee's class paraded through the school. The other children stood and clapped.

Miss Lee's children smiled and smiled. But the biggest smile was at the head of the line. It was Princess Posey, and she was tickled pink.

POSEY'S PAGES

Posey loves making friends
and learning more about new
people. Here are some
questions she'd ask you
if she could:

My first grade parade was so much fun!
What would you wear if your
class had a first grade parade?

I have a stuffed giraffe named Roger
He's white with blue spots. He sleeps
with me every night. Do you have a
favorite stuffed animal? What is its name?
What does it look like?

• • •

I was nervous about starting first grade.
Were you? What were you scared about?
If you're in kindergarten, how do you
feel about first grade?

• • •

I feel special when I wear my pink
tutu, like a brave princess. Do you
have something you wear that
makes you feel special? What is
it? How does it make you feel?

• • •

Someday, I want to ride the bus to school
with my friends. Do you ride the bus?
Is it fun?

• • •

I felt shy when I saw Miss Lee in Hank's store. I wanted to hide. Have you ever seen your teacher outside of school? What did you do?

• • •

Making friends at school is so much fun. Who are some of the friends you've made? What do you like to do together?

• • •

Nick and Tyler tease me a lot. They scared me about the Monster of the Blue Hall. Does anyone you know tease you? What do they tease you about? What do you do?

PRINCESS POSEY
and the
PERFECT PRESENT

Stephanie Greene

ILLUSTRATED BY
Stephanie Roth Sisson

PUFFIN BOOKS
Published by the Penguin Group
Penguin Group (USA) LLC
375 Hudson Street
New York, New York 10014

USA * Canada * UK * Ireland * Australia
New Zealand * India * South Africa * China

penguin.com
A Penguin Random House Company

First published simultaneously in the United States of America by G. P. Putnam's Sons
and Puffin Books, divisions of Penguin Young Readers Group, 2011
This omnibus edition published by Puffin Books,
an imprint of Penguin Young Readers Group, 2014

Text copyright © 2011 by Stephanie Greene
Illustrations copyright © 2011 by Stephanie Roth Sisson

THE LIBRARY OF CONGRESS HAS CATALOGED THE G. P. PUTNAM'S SONS EDITION AS FOLLOWS:
Green, Stephanie.
Princess Posey and the perfect present / by Stephanie Greene ;
illustrated by Stephanie Roth Sisson.
p.   cm.
Summary: For first-grader Posey, every school day is great until her teacher's birthday, when
her best friend's gift of an enormous bouquet puts Posey's few, home-grown roses to shame.
ISBN: 978-0-399-25462-8 (hardcover)
[1. Teachers—Fiction. 2. Schools—Fiction. 3. Best friends—Fiction. 4. Friendship—Fiction.]
I. Sisson, Stephanie Roth, ill. II. Title
PZ7.G8434Pri2011
[Fic]—dc22 2010001276

Puffin Books ISBN 978-0-14-241828-4

This omnibus edition ISBN 978-0-14-751472-1

Printed in the United States of America

1 3 5 7 9 10 8 6 4 2

To Lily,
the family's newest princess
—S.G.

To Kathy Foster,
an amazing teacher at
Bellevue-Santa Fe Charter School
—S.R.S.

CONTENTS

HAPPY WALKING

"Remember when I was afraid to walk into school by myself?" said Posey. "I was silly, wasn't I, Mom?"

Her mom stopped the car in front of the school.

1

"You weren't silly," she said. "You were just out of kindergarten."

The girls in Posey's class said the word *silly* all the time. Sometimes it meant "funny." Other times it meant "babyish."

"I bet Danny will be afraid to walk into school by himself, won't he?" said Posey.

Her baby brother kicked his feet against his car seat and reached out his hand.

Posey shook it.

"Danny's lucky," her mom said.

"He has a big sister to show him
how."

Posey got out of the car and shut
the door. "See you later, alligator,"
she called.

"After a while, crocodile," her mom called back.

Posey walked into the school and down to the blue hall. Miss Lee was standing outside their classroom door.

"Miss Lee!" Posey called. "Hi, Miss Lee!"

She knew children were supposed to walk in the halls at Middle Pond School.

Not run.

But Posey couldn't help it. When she saw her very own teacher

standing outside their door, she
started to skip.

She was careful to skip her tiny
inside skip. Not her big outside skip.
Besides, skipping wasn't running. It
was happy walking.

And Posey was happy.

She loved her big classroom where
she could see all her friends.

She loved having
her own cubby
with her
name
over it.

She loved raising her hand when she knew the answer to a question. And she loved her two best friends, Ava and Nikki.

But most of all, Posey loved her teacher, Miss Lee.

ANOTHER
GREAT DAY

"**G**ood morning, Posey," Miss Lee said. "You're very cheerful this morning."

"See my new kitty eraser?" said Posey.

"It's very nice," said Miss Lee. "Make sure you keep it in your cubby."

"I will." Posey pulled a piece of paper out of her backpack. "Look what I made for you."

"Another drawing?" Miss Lee shook her head. "I don't know how you find time to sleep."

Posey laughed. She loved it when Miss Lee teased her.

"It's a pink rainbow!" Miss Lee sounded amazed.

"I used three different pinks," Posey said.

"I see that." Miss Lee smiled. "I have never seen a rainbow like this before."

"It's the only one in the world," said Posey.

"In that case, I think we need to hang it in our gallery, don't you?" said Miss Lee.

"Oh, yes!"

That was exactly what Posey had hoped Miss Lee was going to

The Learners' Gallery

say. The Learners' Gallery was where they hung special stories and drawings.

Their class was called "Miss Lee's Learners."

Learning was very important work.

In first grade they learned new things all day long.

How to spell new words. How to write stories. How to add numbers like two plus three.

Posey was proud to be one of Miss Lee's Learners. She was excited to have her drawing hang in the Learners' Gallery, too.

"There. How's that?" Miss Lee stood back to admire Posey's picture.

"Beautiful," said Posey.

She went to her cubby and put away her things. She looked around for Ava and Nikki. There they were, in front of the word wall! Posey saw Ava's blond curls and Nikki's black ones.

"Hi, Ava! Hi, Nikki!" Posey skipped over to them. "How do you like my new kitty eraser?"

"I wish I had one," said Nikki.

"Maybe you can try mine tomorrow," said Posey.

"Can I try it, too?" Ava asked.

"Okay."

The three friends hugged.

It was going to be another great day in first grade.

CHAPTER THREE

"WHOOSH!"

Gramps picked up Posey after school. There was a bag of mulch in the back of his truck.

"I bet today is gardening day," Posey said.

"How did you get to be so smart?" said Gramps. "I promised your mom I would get her flower beds ready for winter."

"Can I help?" asked Posey.

"I'm counting on it," Gramps said.

After Posey had her snack, she went to her room to put on her pink tutu. It was her favorite thing to wear.

She never told anyone, but when she wore her pink tutu, she was Princess Posey, the Pink Princess.

Princess Posey could go anywhere and do anything.

Especially if she had her magic
princess wand. Posey picked it up.

She had made it herself with a
stick and tinfoil.

It had a star at the end, too.

Posey waved it in the air as she
ran outside. She was going to use it
now to help the flowers grow.

The yellow flowers were first.

"Whoosh!" Princess Posey made
her magic wand noise and waved it
over the flowers. "I hereby com-
mand you to grow!" she said.

"Whoosh!" Posey commanded
the blue flowers.

"Whoosh!" she told the white flowers.

The pink roses were last. They were her favorite. She had helped Gramps plant them.

"You are the most beautifulest flowers in the whole garden," she said.

"Whoosh!"

"Hey!" Gramps called. He was kneeling on the grass beside a pile of mulch. "Where's my best helper?"

Posey ran over to him. "I was playing a game," she said.

"I figured as much." Gramps held out his hand. "I wanted you to see this before it flew away."

A ladybug with four black dots was crawling in the palm of Gramps's hand.

"It means good luck, doesn't it?" said Posey.

"Sure does," said Gramps.

25

"Ladybug,
ladybug, fly
away home,"
Posey said.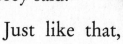

Just like that,
the ladybug opened
its wings and lifted into the air.

"I guess you told it a thing or
two," said Gramps. "Dig in."

Posey scooped up two handfuls
of mulch. "I'll make sure the roses
are warm," she said.

"That's my girl," Gramps said.
"They will thank you for it, too."

CHAPTER
FOUR

MISS LEE'S NEWS

At the end of school the next day, Miss Lee called, "Boys and girls. I have a special announcement."

A special announcement! Posey put down her pencil. Everyone around her did, too.

"Guess what tomorrow is?" Miss Lee asked.

"Wednesday!" Luca shouted.

Posey frowned. That Luca! He always forgot to raise his hand. Miss Lee usually reminded him. All she did now was smile.

"That's right, Luca. It's Wednesday," she said. "But it's also my birthday."

Miss Lee's birthday! How exciting!

"It's my turn to bring in birthday cupcakes," Miss Lee said. "We'll celebrate after lunch."

Everyone started to talk. The room buzzed like the inside of a beehive. Posey got in line with Ava and Nikki to wait for the bell.

"I'm going to bring Miss Lee a present," Nikki said.

"Me too," said Ava. "I'm going to bring her something very special!"

"I'm going to bring her something very, very special!" said Nikki. "How about you, Posey?"

Posey knew exactly what she was going to bring. Her present was going to be very, very, *very* special.

31

CHAPTER FIVE

THE VERY, VERY, VERY SPECIAL PRESENT

"**H**urry, Danny, hurry!" Posey cried. She ran across the backyard.

"He's coming as fast as he can," her mom said. She held Danny's hand to keep him from falling.

Danny couldn't walk by himself yet. All he did was stumble and fall, stumble and fall.

Every time he fell on his bottom, he laughed. Most of the time Posey laughed with him.

Today she wanted him to go faster.

"See, Mom?" Posey said. She waited for them in front of the roses. "One, two, three, four, five! Miss Lee will love them, won't she?"

"I'm sure she will," said her mom.

"Let's leave this one." Posey
pointed to a tiny bud. It was still
closed. "It hasn't been born yet."

"Maybe we should cut them in
the morning," said her mom.

"Danny might spill his cereal

in the morning," said Posey. "We
might be late."

"Okay."

Her mom cut the roses. Posey
carried them inside. She wrapped
the stems in a wet paper towel.

Then she wrapped foil around the paper towel and put the roses in the refrigerator.

"I bet no one else gives Miss Lee such a special present," she said. "She'll be amazed, won't she, Mom?"

"She'll love them because you grew them," said her mom.

Posey could hardly wait to see Miss Lee's face. She was going to smile and smile.

She would know Posey liked her more than anyone.

In her secret heart, Posey hoped Miss Lee would like her more than anyone, too.

CHAPTER SIX

A
NOT-SO-WONDERFUL
SURPRISE

Posey held her roses tight as she walked slowly down the blue hall. She didn't skip even her tiny inside skip.

Excitement butterflies were tickling the inside of her stomach.

Miss Lee was going to be so happy. She was going to say, "Why, Posey! These are the most beautiful flowers I ever saw!"

But that's not what Miss Lee said.

When Posey got to the door of their classroom, she heard Miss Lee say, "Why, Nikki! What beautiful flowers!"

Oh, no!

Posey stopped.

Miss Lee and Nikki were standing by Miss Lee's desk. Miss Lee was holding the biggest bunch of flowers Posey had ever seen.

They were every color. They were wrapped in beautiful green paper.

The paper was tied with glittery ribbons that curled at the ends.

"We got them in a store that had nothing but flowers," Nikki said.

"It's called a florist," said Miss Lee. "We'll put that word on the word wall today."

She smiled at Nikki. Nikki smiled back.

Posey's heart felt like it was being squeezed.

"I have just the thing for them!"

Miss Lee said. She went to her closet and took out a vase. "How would you like to fill it with water for me?"

"Sure!" said Nikki.

Nikki filled Miss Lee's "just the thing!" vase with water. After Miss Lee put in the flowers, she wound the glittery ribbons around her wrist like a bracelet.

She and Nikki laughed.

Posey's mouth felt trembly. Her eyes felt hot. Quiet as a mouse, she went back into the hall.

Nikki's flowers were so beautiful!
Posey couldn't give five little roses
that were wrapped in a soggy paper
towel to Miss Lee now.

Yesterday they looked so beautiful. Today they looked so small.

The tinfoil was crumpled where Posey had gripped it. One of the roses had a droopy head like it was sleepy.

Looking at them made Posey feel sad.

She put them in her backpack. She zipped it closed.

Now Miss Lee wouldn't know how much Posey liked her.

Now she would like Nikki more than she liked Posey.

CHAPTER
SEVEN

"YOU'RE NOT MY FRIEND"

Ava and Nikki rushed up to Posey's table.

"Miss Lee loved the story I wrote for her!" Ava said.

"She loved my flowers, too!" said Nikki. "What did you give her, Posey?"

"I don't like you anymore, Nikki," Posey said with her trembly mouth. "You're not my friend."

Nikki's eyes got big the way they did when she was going to cry.

Posey turned around in her chair so she couldn't see. Being mean made her feel a little better.

But not for long.

She didn't have anyone to share her cookies with at lunch. She sat by herself on the swings at recess.

When Miss Lee asked for helpers to pass out her birthday cupcakes, Posey didn't raise her hand.

The cupcakes had fluffy white frosting. They were covered with colored sprinkles.

Posey didn't touch hers.

Miss Lee walked around the room. She stopped at every table.

"Aren't you going to eat yours?" she said when she got to Posey.

Posey shook her head.

"You have been quiet all day," said Miss Lee. "Do you feel all right?"

Posey nodded.

Miss Lee crouched down. "Would you like to talk about it?" she whispered.

Posey shook her head again. This time, she squeezed her eyes shut.

"All right." Miss Lee stood up.

"I'll wrap this so you can take it home."

Posey watched Miss Lee walk away. She *did* want to talk about it. But not with Miss Lee.

With her mom.

Except, when Posey opened the car door after school and her mom said, "How did Miss Lee like your roses?" Posey didn't talk.

She cried.

CHAPTER EIGHT

AS GOOD AS NEW

"There." Posey's mom put the last rose into the jar of water. She had snipped off the tips of each stem so they could drink.

"They will be as good as new in no time," she said.

Posey sniffed. She had told her mom what happened. Except not the part where she was mean to Nikki.

"Can Danny have a piece of your cupcake?" her mom said.

"I guess so."

Her mom put a piece of cupcake on the tray of Danny's high chair. She sat down at the kitchen table next to Posey.

"I'm sorry you were disappointed, Posey," she said. "But you should have given Miss Lee your flowers."

"Nikki's not my friend anymore," Posey said.

"You're being silly." Her mom tucked a piece of hair behind Posey's ear. "Nikki didn't know you were bringing flowers, did she?"

"No."

Posey had kept her idea a secret, but Nikki came up with it, too. They came up with the same good idea lots of times. That's why they were best friends.

She had hurt the feelings of one her own best friends.

Posey's mouth got trembly again.

"But she gave Miss Lee about fifty hundred," she said.

"The number doesn't matter," her mom said. "Look at Danny!

We only have one of him and that's plenty, don't you think?"

When Posey and her mom looked at him, Danny laughed.

He had frosting all over his face. One blue sprinkle sat on the tip of his nose. He was spreading more frosting on the tray of his high chair.

"If we had more than one Danny, the house would be a mess!" Posey said.

"Exactly." Her mom laughed as she stood up. "You go get changed while I clean him up," she said. "We'll play outside for a bit."

"But how will Miss Lee know I like her?" Posey said.

"You'll find a way to show her," her mom said. "Your very own Posey way."

CHAPTER
NINE

SILLY POSEY!

Posey put on her pink tutu. She also put on her pink veil. It always made her feel better.

Gramps gave
it to her for
the first day
of first grade.
It was covered
with stars.

Posey went outside.
The sun was
warm on
her face. She
closed her eyes
and held out
her arms.

She was Princess Posey.

Princess Posey was lying on a soft pink cloud. The cloud was slowly drifting across the sky. A striped pink rainbow curved high above her head.

The stars on her veil sparkled in the sun.

Princess Posey was beautiful and kind. She wouldn't cry if someone gave the same present. She would just think of another present.

An even more special present.

Of course!

Posey opened her eyes. She stamped her foot.

You're a *silly* Posey, she told herself.

All she had to do was think of another present.

An after-birthday present! That was it! Miss Lee probably never got an after-birthday present before.

What could she bring? Where could it be?

Posey suddenly saw it.

The tiny rose that was left on the bush had opened in the night.

Today was the rose's birthday, too!

Posey crept close and saw the most amazing thing. A ladybug had crawled inside. It was nestled between the petals, fast asleep.

"Ladybug, ladybug, don't fly away home," Posey whispered. "I'm taking you to school tomorrow."

CHAPTER TEN

JUST THE THING
FOR IT!

Posey tiptoed down the hall to her classroom. She didn't make a peep. The ladybug stayed fast asleep.

"Hi, Miss Lee," she said.

Miss Lee spun around. "Oh, Posey!" she said. "You were so quiet that I didn't hear you come in."

"I brought you an after-birthday present," said Posey. She held out the rose. "Yesterday was its birthday, too."

"I've never gotten an after-birthday present before," Miss Lee said. "It's beautiful."

"It will bring you good luck," said Posey.

"It will?"

"Look." Posey pointed at the ladybug.

"Oh, my." Miss Lee sounded amazed. "I think it might be the

only lucky, after-birthday rose in
the world, don't you?"

"It is," said Posey.

"I have just the thing for it!" Miss Lee went to her closet and took out a small thin vase. "It's called a bud vase," she said. "It only holds one flower."

"Two would be crowded," said Posey.

"Exactly." Miss Lee smiled. "Would you like to fill it with water for me?"

"Okay."

Posey filled the vase with water. Miss Lee put in the rose.

It was a perfect fit.

"I feel lucky already to have

a girl as thoughtful as you in my class, Posey," Miss Lee said. "Thank you."

"You're welcome."

Posey went to her cubby and put away her pack. Ava and Nikki were sitting on the floor in the reading corner.

"Can I play?" Posey said.

"You were mean to me," Nikki told her.

"I'm sorry. I was being silly." Posey sat down next to her. "You can use my kitty eraser today."

"Okay," said Nikki.

"Can I use it, too?" asked Ava.

"You can share it," Posey told her.

"We're playing family," Nikki said. "We're both mothers and our babies are asleep."

"I'll be the baby that woke up," Posey said. "Wah-wah!" She crawled onto Nikki and Ava's laps.

"Oh, Posey, you're so silly," Nikki said.

"Wah-wah," said Posey. "Me have wet diaper."

"Posey!" Ava cried.

Nikki and Posey giggled.

It was going to be another great day in first grade.

POSEY'S PAGES

Make your own magic
princess wand! All you need
is aluminum foil, a piece of
cardboard, a pair of scissors,
and a stick about the size
of a pencil.

1. Tear off a piece of foil that's three
inches wide. Wrap it around your stick.

2. Draw a star on the piece of
cardboard and cut it out.

3. Tear off a large piece of foil. Cut it into strips that are about a half inch wide.

4. Put the top of your stick in the middle of the star. Wrap the foil strips around the points of the star and then around the stick until the star is secure.

5. Wrap your star in another piece of foil to cover all of the strips.

Decorate your wand with sparkly glue, stickers, or ribbons, if you want. My wand goes WHOOSH! What sound does yours make?

PRINCESS POSEY
and the
NEXT-DOOR DOG

Stephanie Greene

ILLUSTRATED BY
Stephanie Roth Sisson

PUFFIN BOOKS
Published by the Penguin Group
Penguin Group (USA) LLC
375 Hudson Street
New York, New York 10014

USA * Canada * UK * Ireland * Australia
New Zealand * India * South Africa * China

penguin.com
A Penguin Random House Company

First published simultaneously in the United States of America by G. P. Putnam's Sons
and Puffin Books, divisions of Penguin Young Readers Group, 2011
This omnibus edition published by Puffin Books,
an imprint of Penguin Young Readers Group, 2014

THE LIBRARY OF CONGRESS HAS CATALOGED THE G. P. PUTNAM'S SONS EDITION AS FOLLOWS:
Greene, Stephanie.
Princess Posey and the next-door dog / by Stephanie Greene ;
illustrated by Stephanie Roth Sisson.
p.   cm.
Summary: Holding her princess wand, six-year-old Posey finds the courage
to visit the large dog next door.
ISBN: 978-0-399-25463-5 (hardcover)
[1. Dogs—Fiction. 2. Fear—Fiction.]
I. Sisson, Stephanie Roth, ill. II. Title.
PZ7.G8434Pq 2011
[Fic]—dc22 2010028012

Puffin Books ISBN 978-0-14-241939-7

This omnibus edition ISBN 978-0-14-751472-1

Printed in the United States of America

1 3 5 7 9 10 8 6 4 2

For Dianne White,
wonderful teacher and friend
—S.G.

For Kenny the pug,
our next-door dog,
and his parents,
Chris and Reed
—S.R.S.

CONTENTS

BIG EXCITEMENT

There was big excitement in Miss Lee's class. Posey ran up to Nikki and Ava as soon as they got to the room.

"Luca has a new puppy!" she said. "Come see the picture!"

1

There was a crowd of children around Luca. Everyone was pushing to be in front.

"Let me see!" they all said. "Let me look!"

"He's so cute," said Posey. "Wait till you see."

But Ava and Nikki didn't get to see.

Miss Lee clapped her hands. "Boys and girls," she called in her pay-attention voice. "I need all of you to sit at your tables, please."

Everyone hurried to sit down.

"I know you're excited about Luca's puppy," Miss Lee said. "So we will hold our class meeting now. He can tell us about it."

All of the kids sat in a circle on the rug in front of the Word Wall. Miss Lee sat in her rocking chair.

"Remember the rule," she told
them. "We only ask questions about
Luca's dog. We don't tell stories
about our own pets. This is Luca's
time to share."

It was a hard rule to follow. Everyone wanted to talk about their pets, too.

"Go ahead, Luca," said Miss Lee.

Luca stood up. "I got a new puppy," he said.

He held
up a picture. It was
a little dog with floppy ears. "His
name is Roscoe. He's brown."

Posey rose up on her knees so
she could see better. So did everyone
else.

"Bottoms, please." Miss Lee
waited until they all settled down.
Then she said, "Who would like to
ask Luca a question?"

Hands shot into the air.

"Nate?" said Miss Lee.

"What kind of dog is he?" Nate asked.

"A mix," said Luca.

Miss Lee called on Maya next.

"Where does he sleep?" she asked.

"In his crate," Luca said.

"Does he cry at night?" Nikki asked.

"Sometimes," Luca answered.

There were so many questions, they ran out of time.

"We have to stop now," said Miss Lee. "It's time for reading."

"Ohhh..." A disappointed sound went up around the circle.

"Here's what we'll do." Miss Lee stood up. "You are all very interested in dogs. So this week, you can write a story about your own dog or pet. Then you can read it to the class."

Everyone got excited again.

Except Posey. She didn't have a pet.

Not a dog.

Not a cat.

Not a hamster.

"Those of you who don't have a

8

pet," Miss Lee said, "can write about the pet you hope to own someday."

Miss Lee had saved the day!

Now Posey had something to write about, too.

PAINS IN
THE NECK

Posey told her mom about Luca's puppy on the way home.

"Everyone in my class has a pet except me," she said.

"I'm sure not everyone," said her mom.

"Well, lots of kids." The ends of Posey's mouth turned down.

"We have talked about this before," her mom said. She parked their car next to the house. "No pets until Danny gets bigger. I have enough to take care of as it is."

Danny was in his car seat next to her. Posey looked at him and frowned.

He wet his diapers. He spit out his vegetables. He made messes.

It was all Danny's fault.

When her mom opened her car door, Posey reached over and pulled his binkie out of his mouth. She hid it behind her back.

Danny let out a roar.

"Posey . . . ?" said her mom.

Posey gave it back to him.
"Sorry, Danny."

Her mom lifted Danny
out of his car seat.
"Maybe you need
some time by
yourself," she said.

Posey went and
sat on her swing.
She didn't pump.
She made marks
in the dirt with
the tip of her
sneaker.

"Hey, Posey!"
a voice called. It was Tyler. He
lived next door. He was playing
soccer with his brother, Nick.

Tyler was in the fourth grade.
Nick was in second. They teased her

all the time. But maybe today they were going to let her play!

Posey ran into their yard.

"You're a big kid now, right?" Nick asked.

"Right," said Posey. "I'm in first grade."

"I don't know," said Tyler. "You still look pretty small to me."

Posey stood up as straight as she could. "I'm bigger than I look," she said.

"Okay." Tyler pointed. "Go stand over there."

Posey ran and stood near a big tree. "Here?" she asked.

"Perfect," said Nick. "Now, don't move."

He and Tyler kicked the ball back and forth. They ran around the yard. They shouted to each other.

"What about me?" Posey called.

"Don't move!" said Tyler.

He gave a great kick. The ball zoomed past Posey. It went into the bushes.

"Game's over!" he shouted. "I win!"

"But I didn't get to do anything," said Posey.

"Sure you did," said Tyler. "You were a great goalpost."

He and Nick slapped each other on the back and laughed.

"Big dummy heads!" Posey shouted.

She marched home. She would do something to show them she was a big kid.

Just wait!

CHAPTER THREE

AN ALIVE PET

The next day, Maya was the first one to read her story to the class.

"My dog is Dash. He chews socks," she read. "One time he chewed my dad's slipper. Now it's Dash's slipper."

She showed them a picture. It was a yellow dog. It had something blue in its mouth.

"That's a good story, Maya," said Miss Lee. "You told us a lot. Anyone else?"

The rest of the class was still working on their stories.

Posey could not get her story started. She wanted to write about a dog, too. But she had a secret.

She was a tiny bit afraid of dogs.

When she was little, a dog jumped on her in the park. It wanted to lick her ice cream cone

and it knocked her
down.

Posey could still
remember the scary
feeling. She didn't
want anyone to
know.

"I'm writing
about my cat, Puffy,"
Ava said. "She's so soft."

"I'm writing about my gerbil,"
said Nikki. "What are you writing
about, Posey?"

"Why don't you write about
Roger?" said Ava.

Roger was Posey's
stuffed giraffe. He
was blue and white.
She got him when
she was a tiny baby.

But he was not alive.

Posey wanted to write about an
alive pet like everyone else.

"Maybe I'm going to get a real
pet," she said.

"Really?" said Nikki. "When?"

"Maybe soon," Posey pretended.

She would wish and wish.

Maybe it would come true.

CHAPTER FOUR

THE NEXT-DOOR
DOG

Gramps drove Posey home from school. A moving truck was parked in front of the red house next door.

"Looks like you have new neighbors," Gramps said.

"Maybe they have a little girl!" said Posey.

She ran up to her room and put on her pink tutu. She put on her necklace with the pink beads, too. And her magic veil with the stars.

Then she went outside and sat on her swing.

There was a hedge between her yard and the red house. Posey pumped hard so she could see over.

If she went high enough, maybe she'd see a little girl! Maybe the little girl would see her!

See her, Princess Posey, in her beautiful pink tutu. It fluttered up and down with every swing.

But all Posey saw was an empty yard. She stopped pumping.

That's when Posey heard a sound.

Woof . . . Woof . . . Woof.

A dog!

The people next door had a dog! Maybe she could write her story about it!

Posey was so excited, she stopped the swing.

Woof! . . . Woof! . . . WOOF!

Posey froze. It sounded like a big dog.

A very big dog.

WOOF!...WOOF!...WOOF!

And it had a very deep voice.

Like a giant's voice.

Posey's eyes opened wide.

What if it was a giant dog? A giant, jumpy dog like the one in the park? And it didn't like little girls?

WOOF! ... WOOF! ...

Posey didn't wait to hear the third giant WOOF!

She ran.

CHAPTER
FIVE

YOU CAN'T TELL
A DOG BY ITS BARK

Tyler and Nick
were getting on
their bikes in
their driveway.

"Hey, Posey!" Tyler called. "What's your hurry?"

"Did you see a monster?" shouted Nick.

Posey didn't stop. She ran up the steps and into the house.

She slammed the kitchen door behind her. Gramps was standing at the stove.

She was safe.

"Is someone after you?" Gramps asked.

He cooked dinner for them every Wednesday. Posey's mom had to work late. Tonight, he was making chili.

The kitchen smelled good. Posey's heart slowed down.

"Gramps, can a little dog have a big bark?" she asked.

"The only little dogs I know are yappers," said Gramps. "Yap, yap, yap, all day long."

"Big dogs are mean, aren't they?" said Posey.

"Not on your life." Gramps dumped a can of beans into the pot. "I had a dog as big as a horse when I was your age. Target was his name. Target's heart was as big as he was."

"They sure *sound* scary."

"Barks don't mean a thing," Gramps said. "If you want to know about a dog, look at its eyes. Kind eyes mean a kind dog."

Posey shivered. She was too afraid to get close enough to the next-door dog to see its eyes.

"Why the questions about dogs all of a sudden?" said Gramps.

Posey told him about the barks.

"I'll tell you what," Gramps said. "You and your mom can go over there on Saturday. You can meet the dog together."

It was a perfect idea. Posey was so lucky to have her gramps.

She threw her arms
around him. She squeezed
as hard as she could.
"I love you, Gramps,"
she said.

"I love you, too," said Gramps. "But watch I don't get chili on your head."

CHAPTER SIX

NOW OR NEVER

Posey told Ava and Nikki about the barks the next day.

"How are you going to write a story about that dog?" asked Ava. "You don't know what it looks like."

"And you don't know what its name is," said Nikki.

"Maybe it's a ghost dog." Ava opened her eyes wide. "Maybe it isn't even real."

"Maybe you heard a ghost bark," said Nikki.

The three girls shivered. They grabbed one another's hands.

"The ghost dog said woof . . . woof . . . wooooooooooffff!" Posey made it sound like a ghost.

Ava and Nikki shrieked. It was so much fun to be scared when they were together.

"All right, girls. Settle down," Miss Lee called.

Nikki ran over to her.

"Miss Lee!" she said. "Posey has a ghost dog next door!"

"You three are being silly," said Miss Lee. "But that reminds me."

She smiled around at the class.

"Tomorrow will be the last day to read your pet stories," she told them. "Everyone needs to finish up today."

Oh, no!

That meant Posey couldn't wait until Saturday. She had to meet her next-door dog today.

Besides, if she went with her mom, Nick and Tyler would think she was a baby.

She had to do it by herself.

Posey made up her mind right then and there.

She was going to go over and see that giant dog as soon as she got home.

BEING BRAVE

Posey was
ready.

She had on her pink tutu and her magic veil. Posey put on her new belt with purple flowers, too. She held her princess wand in one hand in case she needed magic.

She was Princess Posey.

Princess Posey was brave. She could go anywhere and do anything.

All by herself.

Posey went downstairs. Her mom was folding clean clothes.

"I'm going outside," Posey said.

"Okay," said her mom. "I'll be out in a little bit with Danny."

Posey stood on the back steps and listened. She didn't hear a sound.

Maybe the next-door dog was taking a nap.

That was it!

She would be as quiet as a mouse and peek through the hedge. She could see how big it was without waking it up.

Taking tiny baby steps, Posey tiptoed over to the hedge and looked.

There was a doghouse in the yard behind the red house. It had a fence around it.

Posey heard a small Woof! . . . Woof! . . . Whimper.

What was that?

That's not what it sounded like yesterday.

It sounded like a dog that was crying.

Woof! . . . Whimper . . . whimper.

It was crying!

What if it was hurt? What if it needed her help?

Posey ran all the way around the hedge and into the yard next door. Then she stopped.

A brown dog was lying inside the fence.

It was a giant, all right. It had so much fur, it looked like a bear.

The scared feeling came back to her stomach.

She wanted to help it. She did.

The dog whimpered again.

Whimper . . . whimper . . . whimper.

It was a tiny baby sound. The giant dog didn't seem so giant anymore. It didn't sound as scary, either.

It sounded sad.

Posey tiptoed closer.

No wonder it was crying! Its paw was stuck in one of the holes in the fence. There was dirt all around. The dog had been digging a hole.

The giant dog licked his paw and whimpered.

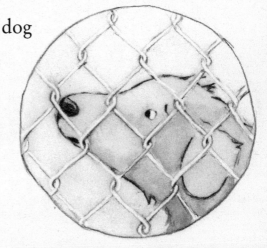

She had to help. She *had* to.

There was only one thing for Posey to do.

CHAPTER EIGHT

HERO'S HERO

Posey crouched down. From here, the brown body looked like a huge mountain.

What if she hurt its paw even more? It might growl at her.

Or bite her, even.

Posey jumped up. She shook her head. She squeezed her eyes shut. No, no, no!

She couldn't do it. She was too afraid. Maybe when she was in second grade.

Then the dog gave a quiet woof!

Posey opened her eyes. The dog was looking up at her. It had huge brown eyes.

They were kind eyes.

Sad eyes.

They looked into Posey's eyes and said, Will you help me?

Yes. Posey made up her mind. She could do it.

She knelt down and took the dog's paw in her hands. "You better not be mean to me," she told it sternly.

Then Posey gently pushed the
paw back through the fence.

The minute it was free, the dog
leaped up.

It shook its big body.

It wagged its long tail.

It wiggled and
waggled and did a
big happy dance.

The dog looked
so funny! It had
dirt on its nose.

The next thing
Posey knew, it licked
her face with its big, slurpy tongue
right through the fence.

Thank you,
thank you,
thank you,
the lick said.

"Yuck," Posey cried. She jumped up. "You have germs, you silly dog."

But she was happy, too.

"He's doing that because you helped him," a voice behind her said. "You're Hero's hero."

CHAPTER NINE

DON'T BE AFRAID

A lady smiled at Posey as she came across the yard. "I'm Mrs. Romero, your new neighbor. What's your name?"

"Posey," she answered. "You live next to me."

"Hello, Posey," said Mrs. Romero. "Hero loves you because you helped him."

Mrs. Romero opened the gate to Hero's pen. Posey followed her in.

"Sit," Mrs. Romero told him.

Hero sat.

"Posey, this is Hero," said Mrs. Romero. "Hero, this is Posey. Shake hands."

Hero held up his paw.

Posey came forward slowly and shook it.

She rested her hand on Hero's broad back. His fur was soft and warm.

"He's just a big baby," Mrs. Romero said. She kissed Hero's

head. "No matter how many times he gets stuck, he keeps trying to dig under fences. Don't you, boy?"

Hero leaned his big body against Posey. She patted his head. When she stopped, he moved his head to ask for more.

"He likes little girls," Posey said.

"Yes, he does," said Mrs. Romero. "He loves all children."

"I'm so glad you moved next door," said Posey.

"Po-sey!" someone called.

It was her mom.

"Can I show Hero to my mom and Danny?" Posey asked.

"Sure. I'll come with you." Mrs. Romero snapped a red leash to Hero's collar. "Would you like to walk him?"

"Oh, can I?"

Posey held Hero's leash and walked him into her yard. He stuck by her side the whole way.

"What a wonderful dog!" her mom said. "Look, Danny! Look what Posey found!"

Danny squealed. He held out his arms.

"His name is Hero," Posey said.

"Posey is *his* hero," said Mrs. Romero. "She unstuck his paw."

Just then, Nick and Tyler came out of their house.

"Can I show them Hero?" Posey asked.

"Go ahead," said Mrs. Romero.

Posey proudly walked Hero across the driveway. Nick ducked behind Tyler when he saw them coming.

"Whoa!" said Tyler. "Is that a bear or a dog?"

"His name is Hero," said Posey. She walked up to them. "His paw was stuck, but I helped him."

"Weren't you afraid?" Tyler asked as he petted Hero's head.

"A little."

"Cool," Tyler said. "See, Nick? Posey doesn't act like a chicken."

Nick stayed behind his brother. Posey could tell he was afraid.

"You can pet him," she told him. "He won't hurt you. He's very gentle. Aren't you, boy?"

She knelt down and wrapped her arms around Hero's neck. He looked at her with his huge brown eyes.

They were filled with love.

They made Posey feel ten feet tall.

She was hugging a dog as big as
a bear.

And she wasn't afraid.

HE'S MY HERO

It was the last day to read pet stories.

"Did you hear the ghost dog again?" Nikki asked Posey.

"He's a real dog," Posey said. "I met him. He's a giant."

"Oh, no!" said Ava. "What did you do? Were you afraid?"

Posey shook her head. She didn't want to tell them. She wanted her story to be a surprise.

"Posey?" Miss Lee said. "You are the last one to read. Are you ready?"

"Yes." Posey picked up her paper. She stood in front of the class.

"Big dogs have big barks," she read. "They go, Woof! . . . Woof! . . . WOOF!"

Everyone laughed.

"A dog moved next door to me."
Posey held her paper tight. "He is
big. But he is gentle."

Last night, she did not know how to spell *gentle*. Her mom wrote it down for her.

"His paw was stuck in the fence. I pushed it out," Posey read. "Tyler said, 'Cool.'"

She turned her paper around so everyone could see the picture she drew.

"This is my next-door dog," she told them. "He helped me be brave. He's my hero."

P❀SEY'S PAGES

I made my own beaded necklace. It was so easy. All you need is a pencil; scissors; glue; a piece of yarn, elastic, or string long enough for a necklace; and bright-colored paper (magazines, wrapping paper, wallpaper).

1. Cut the paper into long, skinny triangles that are about one inch wide at the base.

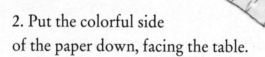

2. Put the colorful side of the paper down, facing the table.

3. Lay the pencil along the base of a triangle.

4. Hold the edge of the paper to the pencil and roll the pencil over one and a half times.

PRINCESS
POSEY
and the
FIRST GRADE
BOYS

Stephanie Greene

ILLUSTRATED BY
Stephanie Roth Sisson

PRINCESS
POSEY
FIRST
GRADER
and the
VALENTINE'S
DAY
BALLET

Stephanie Greene

ILLUSTRATED BY
Stephanie Roth Sisson